Count Magnus

*A Gothic Horror Classic of Ancient
Evil
and Forbidden Curiosity*

A Modern Translation

Adapted for the Contemporary Reader

M.R. James

Translated by Tim Zengerink

Table of Contents

Preface - Message to the Reader

What If You Could Help Rebuild the Greatest Library in Human History?

Thousands of years ago, the Library of Alexandria stood as the crown jewel of human achievement — a sanctuary where the collected wisdom of every known civilization was gathered, preserved, and shared freely.

And then, it was lost.

Through fire, conquest, and the slow erosion of time, humanity lost not just books — but ideas, dreams, discoveries, and stories that could have changed the world forever.

Today, the Library of Alexandria lives again — and you are invited to be a part of its restoration.

Our mission is simple yet profound:

To rebuild the greatest library the world has ever known, and to translate all timeless works into every language and dialect, so that no seeker of knowledge is ever left behind again.

By joining our movement to rebuild the modern Library of Alexandria, you become part of an unprecedented mission:

- **Unlimited Access to the Greatest Audiobooks & eBooks Ever Written:**

  Instantly explore thousands of legendary works— Plato, Shakespeare, Jane Austen, Leo Tolstoy, and countless more. All instantly available to read or listen, placing a complete literary universe at your fingertips.

- **Beautiful Paperback & Deluxe Editions at Printing Cost**

  Own any title as an elegant paperback, deluxe hardcover, or stunning collectible boxset—offered to you at true printing cost, delivered straight to your door. Build your personal Library of Alexandria, crafted for beauty, built for durability, and worthy of proud display.

- **Fresh Translations for Modern Readers—in Every Language & Dialect**

  Enjoy timeless masterpieces reimagined in clear, contemporary language—no more outdated phrases or obscure references. Alongside the original versions, we're tirelessly translating these classics into every language and dialect imaginable, ensuring accessibility and understanding across cultures and generations.

- **Join a Global Renaissance of Literature & Knowledge**

  You directly support expanding our library, publishing deluxe editions at true cost, translating works into all global languages, and bringing humanity's greatest stories to people everywhere. By joining today, you're not just preserving a legacy of masterpieces; you set in motion a powerful wave of literary accessibility.

Become a Torchbearer of Knowledge.

Join us for free now at **LibraryofAlexandria.com**

Together, we will ensure that the light of human wisdom never fades again.

With gratitude and a shared love of knowledge,

The Modern Library of Alexandria Team

Visit:

www.libraryofalexandria.com

Or scan the code below:

Introduction

The Scholar, the Sarcophagus, and the Unknowable Dread Beneath

M.R. James's Count Magnus, first published in 1904 in the seminal collection Ghost Stories of an Antiquary, stands as one of his most evocative and terrifying supernatural tales. It is, by James's own standards, one of the few stories in which he allows the horror to remain truly unleashed. Where other tales suggest and imply, Count Magnus dares to reveal just enough of its monstrous entity to freeze the imagination. And yet, even in this glimpse, James maintains his signature technique: restraint, ambiguity, and a masterful use of dread grounded in history, landscape, and the frailty of human curiosity.

The story follows Mr. Wraxall, an English travel writer, who journeys to Sweden to research old churches and local traditions for a travel book. A curious and methodical man, Wraxall becomes intrigued by the cryptic legacy of Count Magnus de la Gardie, a 17th-century nobleman whose black-cloaked presence looms over the local region. Through snippets of village gossip, strange historical records, and a foreboding locked sarcophagus, Wraxall uncovers a disturbing legacy of alchemy, cruelty, and occult experimentation. As he digs deeper, it becomes clear that Count Magnus is no mere historical figure—he is a presence that endures. What follows is one of the most chilling supernatural pursuits in literature, culminating in a fatal and unforgettable confrontation.

Count Magnus is widely regarded as one of James's darkest and most atmospheric tales. It merges antiquarian scholarship with cosmic horror, ghostly vengeance, and the suggestion of forces that not only transcend death but also defy understanding. More than just a tale of haunting, it is a meditation on forbidden knowledge, intellectual arrogance, and the mortal cost of curiosity. The story reflects James's lifelong belief that some doors should not be opened—some names should not be spoken—and that there are ancient powers waiting patiently for the naïve to summon them.

This introduction explores the construction, themes, and deeper implications of Count Magnus, including James's approach to antiquarian horror, the role of hidden histories, and the terrifying interplay between scholarship and the supernatural. It will also situate the story within James's broader literary philosophy and its continued relevance in modern horror. In Count

Magnus, we see the full potential of Jamesian terror: not loud, not gory, but creeping—silent—inescapable. A shadow that stretches across centuries, waiting for the wrong question to be asked.

The Allure of Forbidden Knowledge: Scholarship as a Path to Doom

As in many of James's tales, the protagonist of Count Magnus is a solitary scholar. Mr. Wraxall is well-read, disciplined, and professionally curious—precisely the type of character James so often dooms. He is not evil, nor foolish in the conventional sense, but his compulsion to uncover historical truths makes him blind to the warnings of others and deaf to the intuitive fear that begins to mount around him.

Wraxall's decision to research Count Magnus appears innocent. He is writing a travelogue, after all. Yet James subtly shifts the tone as the investigation progresses. The Count is not simply an eccentric nobleman of centuries past. He is associated with horrific rumors: journeys into "the Black Pilgrimage," deals with demonic entities, and punishments so brutal they live on in whispered legend. But these stories do not deter Wraxall—they intrigue him. The more he learns, the more he wants to learn. In this, James draws on the age-old theme of Faustian ambition: the scholar who seeks knowledge without caution and summons destruction in the process.

Wraxall's downfall is sealed when he insists on seeing the Count's sarcophagus, a sealed tomb housed within the family mausoleum, bound with iron and rivets. Despite being told that no one has ever opened it, and that it is best left alone, Wraxall petitions for the key. He does not force it open—he simply asks, and is granted access. The implication is clear: the powers at work in the story are not merely supernatural but cosmic, attuned to human will. By wanting to see, by willing knowledge into light, Wraxall invites the Count's return.

James's treatment of the supernatural is never random. The horror is always summoned by a moral failing—in this case, the hubris of scholarship untethered from humility. Wraxall believes he is in control, that history can be examined like an artifact. But the past, in Count Magnus, is alive. And it is watching.

This dynamic—where curiosity becomes a trap, and intellectual arrogance a death sentence—is a hallmark of James's work and a critique of his own academic culture. In Count Magnus, the pursuit of history leads not to enlightenment, but to terror. And the final lesson is not about Magnus's past—it is about Wraxall's fate.

Manifest Terror:
Atmosphere, Restraint, and the Horror That Follows

One of the great strengths of Count Magnus is James's unmatched ability to build terror through implication and pacing. The early sections of the story are calm, even leisurely. Wraxall's research is conducted methodically. He visits churches, takes notes, meets with locals. But beneath this mundane surface, something begins to stir. James uses small, unsettling details to shift the mood: the villagers who fall silent when the Count's name is mentioned; the iron-bound sarcophagus in the family vault; the cryptic references to the "Black Pilgrimage" to Chorazin, a cursed city mentioned in the Bible as a place of woe.

When Wraxall finally opens the tomb, James does not describe the contents. Instead, he lets silence—and the suggestion of violation—do the work. From this moment forward, Wraxall is no longer alone. Something is following him. He senses presences. He hears movement. The air around him grows heavy. James refuses to show us the Count directly—until the final moments. Instead, he lets the anticipation fester. The horror in Count Magnus is not in what happens, but in what is coming.

This use of pursuit—the idea that something has been awakened and is now closing the distance—is central to the story's power. Wraxall's letters become increasingly agitated. He feels hunted. In the climactic scene, his body is discovered horribly mutilated, as if by wild animals, locked in his room, with claw marks and deep lacerations described in clinical detail by a coroner's report. James never tells us precisely what killed him. But we know. The Count has risen.

What's more horrifying is the suggestion that the Count did not return alone. Earlier in the story, two figures are seen approaching Wraxall's inn. One is tall and shrouded. The other is shorter, cloaked, silent. James never names them, but the implication is that the Count brought something—or someone—back with him from the Black Pilgrimage. The number of rivets removed from the sarcophagus suggests more than one occupant. This final, unanswered detail lingers, like the last line of a curse: open one door, and another opens behind it.

James's restraint is his brilliance. He never tells us what the Black Pilgrimage entails. He never fully explains Count Magnus's nature. The horror is not in the explanation, but in the absence of one. By leaving space for the imagination, James ensures the story will never settle into comfort. The reader is left, like Wraxall, grasping for meaning in the dark.

Count Magnus and the Legacy of Antiquarian Horror

Count Magnus is often cited as one of the earliest and most effective examples of cosmic horror—a form of supernatural fiction that deals not with ghosts and vampires, but with unknowable forces beyond human comprehension. Decades before H.P. Lovecraft would popularize the term, M.R. James wrote stories in which ancient evils were not moral or mythological, but existential. In Count Magnus, the villain is not a ghost seeking justice or a spirit driven by unfinished business. He is a power—sleeping, waiting, malevolent.

The story also exemplifies James's core principles for ghost fiction, which he laid out in lectures and essays: the importance of a familiar setting, the gradual escalation of fear, the use of scholarly protagonists, and the avoidance of overexplanation. These principles would shape not only British horror literature, but also radio, television, and film. The 1971 BBC adaptation of

Count Magnus, though loose in its fidelity, remains a haunting tribute to James's vision, and the story continues to influence writers of quiet, psychological horror to this day.

More broadly, Count Magnus is a warning tale. It reminds us that some truths are better left buried, that curiosity can be a form of hubris, and that the past is not inert. It lives in language, in relics, in names. And sometimes, it waits. Not out of malice, but out of inevitability. The Count does not chase Wraxall—he comes for him. Slowly. Inevitably. Because Wraxall called.

This is the enduring terror of Count Magnus. It is not simply that something ancient was awakened. It is that Wraxall invited it—and had no idea what he was inviting. In the end, he becomes part of the history he once sought to document. He becomes a footnote. A cautionary tale.

And the Count? He waits again, behind the iron and the stone. For the next name. The next question. The next key.

Quis est iste qui venit? Who is this who is coming?

Perhaps it is you.

Count Magnus

How the papers that helped me put this story together ended up in my hands is something I'll explain at the very end. But first, I need to explain what these papers looked like when I got them.

They were partly made up of notes and drafts for a travel book—similar to the kind that was popular in the 1840s and 1850s. One example would be Journal of a Residence in Jutland and the Danish Isles by Horace Marryat. These books usually described trips to little-known places in Europe. They were often filled with drawings or engraved illustrations, and included details like hotel reviews, travel routes, and long conversations with friendly locals, chatty innkeepers, or talkative farmers. In short, they were written in a casual, personal style.

At first, the writer of these papers meant to gather material for just that kind of travel book. But as he continued, his writing shifted into a personal story—his own experience—which he recorded almost to the very end.

The writer's name was Mr. Wraxall. Everything I know about him comes from his own notes. From those, I gather that he was an older man with some money and no close family or friends. He didn't seem to have a permanent home in England, and instead stayed in hotels and boarding houses. He may have planned to settle down eventually, but it never happened. He mentioned a few belongings he had stored at the Pantechnicon, a warehouse in London, which was later destroyed by fire in the early 1870s. That may have erased much of his past.

It also appears that Mr. Wraxall had published a book about a vacation he took in Brittany. I can't tell you more than that, though, because no amount of searching has revealed a title. If it was ever published, it may have been done without his name or under a fake one.

From his writing, it's easy to tell he was smart and well-educated. He had almost earned a fellowship at Brasenose College, Oxford. His main flaw, it seems, was being too curious. While that might be a good thing for a traveler, in his case, it led to serious trouble.

On what would be his final trip, he was planning another book. At the time, most English people didn't know much about Scandinavia, and he thought Sweden would be an interesting place to write about. He had probably come across some old Swedish history books or memoirs and decided to mix travel writing with stories about old Swedish families. He got letters of introduction to some important people in Sweden and set off in early summer of 1863.

There's no need to go into detail about his travels through the country or his stay in Stockholm. What matters is that while in the city, a local scholar told him about a valuable collection of old family documents kept at a historic manor house in a region called Vestergothland. That scholar helped Wraxall get permission to look through them.

The manor house, which I'll call Råbäck (though that's not its real name), was one of the finest old homes in the region. A drawing of it from a 1694 book called Suecia antiqua et moderna shows that it still looks much the same today. Built just after 1600, it closely resembled an English manor house from the same period, with red bricks, stone trim, and classic architectural style. It was built by a member of the De la Gardie family, who still owned it when Wraxall visited. I'll refer to them by that name when needed.

The family welcomed Mr. Wraxall warmly and invited him to stay at the house while he worked. But he preferred his independence and worried about his weak Swedish-speaking skills, so he chose to stay at the nearby village inn instead. The inn was simple but comfortable enough, at least in summer. Staying there meant he had to walk less than a mile each day to get to the manor.

The house was surrounded by a park filled with large, old trees. Nearby was a walled garden, and beyond that, a thick forest that bordered one of the many small lakes scattered across the countryside. Past the woods stood the boundary wall of the estate. Just beyond that, up a steep hill covered with rocky soil, stood the local church, surrounded by tall, dark trees.

The church was very unusual from an English point of view. It was low, with rows of wooden pews and several balconies. A brightly painted old organ with silver pipes stood in the western gallery. The ceiling was flat and covered with a dramatic painting of the Last Judgment, showing burning cities, sinking ships, screaming people, and smiling demons. Large brass chandeliers hung from the ceiling, and the pulpit looked like a miniature house, decorated with tiny wooden angels and saints. A wooden stand next to the pulpit held three hourglasses.

You can still find churches like this in Sweden today. But this one was unique because of an added structure. At the eastern end of the north aisle, the builder of the manor house had added a burial chamber for himself and his family. It was an eight-sided building with oval windows and a domed roof topped with a spire shaped like a pumpkin—something Swedish architects often liked. The roof was made of black-painted copper, and the walls, like the church's, were bright white. The burial room had no connection to the main church inside. Instead, it had its own steps and entrance on the north side.

Just past the churchyard, the path led straight to the village, and in only a few minutes, you'd reach the door of the inn.

On his first day staying near Råbäck, Mr. Wraxall found the church door open. He took notes on the inside of the building, which I've already described. However, he couldn't get into the mausoleum. By peeking through the keyhole, he could just barely make out marble statues, copper tombs, and many fancy family symbols. He really wanted the chance to look around inside properly.

The documents he came to study at the manor turned out to be exactly what he needed for his book.

They included old letters, journals, and records from the first owners of the estate. The handwriting was neat and the papers were full of colorful details about everyday life. The first De la Gardie in the records came across as strong and determined. Not long after building the house, the area went through hard times, and some of the local people rose up and attacked nearby homes. The owner of Råbäck helped lead the effort to stop them. The records mentioned public punishments and the execution of some of the leaders, done harshly and without mercy.

A portrait of this man, Count Magnus de la Gardie, was one of the most striking paintings in the house. Mr. Wraxall took a special interest in it after a long day of work. He didn't describe it in much detail, but it clearly left an impression. He wrote that Count Magnus wasn't just unattractive—his face was unusually unpleasant.

That evening, Wraxall had dinner with the family and walked back to the inn under the still-bright evening sky.

"I must remember to ask the church caretaker if he can let me into the mausoleum," he wrote in his notes. "I saw him there tonight, standing on the steps. It looked like he was locking or unlocking the door."

The next morning, Mr. Wraxall spoke with the innkeeper. At first, it surprised me how much he wrote down from their chat, but then I realized he was planning to use this material for a book—one of those travel stories where casual conversations help fill in the background.

His main goal was to find out if any stories about Count Magnus still existed in the village, and if the people had a good or bad opinion of him. What he found was that Count Magnus was not remembered fondly. If his workers arrived late on the days they owed him labor, they were punished—either forced to sit on a wooden horse, whipped, or even branded in the courtyard. There were also rumors of men who had built homes on land that the Count claimed as his own. Mysteriously, their homes burned down one winter night—with their families still inside.

But the detail the innkeeper kept coming back to— the one that seemed to bother him most—was that Count Magnus had taken something called the Black Pilgrimage and brought back a "presence" with him.

Naturally, like Wraxall, you might wonder what the Black Pilgrimage was. But just like him, you'll have to wait for an answer. The innkeeper didn't want to talk about it. In fact, when he was suddenly called away, he seemed glad to have an excuse to leave. He stuck his head back through the door a moment later to say he was going to Skara and wouldn't return until the evening.

So, Mr. Wraxall had no choice but to go about his day as planned. The papers he was working on quickly took his mind off the conversation. They were letters written between Sophia Albertina in Stockholm and her cousin Ulrica Leonora, who lived at Råbäck, between the years 1705 and 1710. These letters were full of interesting insights into life and culture in Sweden at that time. People who have read the full collection published by the Swedish Historical Manuscripts Commission can confirm how fascinating they are.

That afternoon, when he finished with the letters, Wraxall returned the boxes to their proper places on the shelf. Then he began looking through some nearby books to decide what to focus on next. Most of the books on that shelf were old account records written by Count Magnus himself. But one of them stood out—it wasn't an account book, but a collection of writings on alchemy and other unusual subjects, written by someone else in the 1500s.

Since Wraxall didn't know much about alchemy, he probably spent more time than necessary listing out the strange titles he found: The Book of the Phoenix, The Thirty Words, The Book of the Toad, The Book of Miriam, Turba Philosophorum, and others. Then, with great excitement, he found something especially interesting. In the middle of the book, on what had originally been a blank page, there was a short passage written by Count Magnus himself. The heading read: The Book of the Black Pilgrimage.

There were only a few lines, but it was enough to show that the story the innkeeper had hinted at was very old—and Count Magnus had believed in it. Here's what the writing said in English:

"If a man wants to live a long life, to gain a loyal servant, and to see the blood of his enemies, he must first go to the city of Chorazin and there greet the prince…"

One word had been scratched out, but not well enough to hide it. Wraxall was fairly sure the missing word was of the air. That was the end of the note, followed by one more line in Latin: "Seek the rest of this subject among the more secret things."

There's no denying that what Mr. Wraxall found out made Count Magnus seem even stranger and more unsettling. But since he had lived nearly 300 years before, Wraxall wasn't scared—if anything, he thought the Count's interest in alchemy and possibly even magic just made him more fascinating. That night, after spending a long time staring at the Count's portrait in the manor's hallway, Wraxall headed back to the inn. His mind was so focused on Count Magnus that he barely noticed the beautiful evening light or the fresh smell of the woods. He was surprised when he suddenly realized he was already standing at the gate to the churchyard and only a few minutes from dinner. As he looked toward the mausoleum, he said out loud, "Ah, Count Magnus, there you are. I really would like to meet you."

He later wrote, "Like a lot of people who spend time alone, I often talk to myself out loud. And unlike in old myths, I don't expect anyone to answer." Thankfully, there was no voice that responded. The only sound was the clatter of something metal falling to the floor inside the church—probably dropped by a cleaner—which startled him. He added, "I think Count Magnus sleeps just fine."

That same evening, the innkeeper, who had heard Wraxall mention he wanted to meet the church clerk (or deacon, as he's called in Sweden), introduced them in the inn's sitting room. They quickly made plans to visit the De la Gardie family's tomb the next day, and chatted for a bit.

Wraxall remembered that one of a deacon's duties in Scandinavia is to prepare young people for confirmation, so he decided to ask a Bible-related question.

"Do you know anything about Chorazin?" he asked.

The deacon looked surprised but answered right away, saying that Chorazin was one of the towns condemned in the Bible.

"That's right," said Wraxall. "Isn't it in ruins now?"

"I believe so," the deacon replied. "I've heard some of our older priests say the Antichrist is supposed to be born there. And there are stories..."

"What kind of stories?" Wraxall asked quickly.

The deacon paused. "Stories I've forgotten," he said, and soon after, said good night and left.

Now Wraxall was alone with the innkeeper and free to ask more. He wasn't planning to go easy.

"Herr Nielsen," he said, "I found something about the Black Pilgrimage. You might as well tell me what you know. What did Count Magnus bring back with him?"

Swedes are known for taking their time to answer, or maybe the innkeeper was just being extra careful.

Either way, Wraxall noticed that he took nearly a full minute to reply. Then he stepped closer and finally spoke, clearly struggling with the words.

"Mr. Wraxall, I'll tell you one small story, and that's it. Please don't ask anything more after that."

He began his tale.

"Ninety-two years ago, during my grandfather's time, there were two men who said, 'The Count is dead, we don't care about him. Let's go hunt in his woods tonight.' They meant the big forest on the hill behind Råbäck. People warned them not to go. They said, 'You'll meet things that should be resting, not walking.' But the two men just laughed. There were no guards in the woods then, and the family wasn't at home, so they thought they could do whatever they wanted.

That night, they went into the woods. My grandfather was sitting here in this room. It was summer, and the night was light. He had the window open and could see the forest from where he sat.

He was with two or three others. At first, everything was quiet. Then they heard a scream coming from the woods, far away, but clear. It was the kind of scream that sounded like it came from deep inside someone's soul. Everyone in the room grabbed onto each other. They sat like that for about forty-five minutes.

Then they heard laughter—not close, but only about three hundred yards away. It wasn't from either of the two men. In fact, all of them agreed it didn't sound like any human at all. After that, they heard a heavy door slam shut.

When the sun came up, they went to the priest and said, 'Father, please put on your robe and come with us. We need to bury these two men, Anders Bjornsen and Hans Thorbjorn.' They were sure the men were dead.

So they went to the woods. My grandfather never forgot that walk. Everyone looked pale, like they had seen a ghost. The priest was terrified too. He had heard the scream and the laugh and said, 'If I can't forget those sounds, I'll never sleep again.'

They found the two men at the edge of the woods. Hans Thorbjorn was standing up, leaning against a tree, pushing at something with both hands—something no one else could see. He was alive, but clearly not right. They took him to the hospital in Nykjoping, and he died before winter. The whole time, even near the end, he kept pushing at nothing with his hands.

Anders Bjornsen was already dead. He had once been a handsome man, but not anymore. The flesh on his face had been sucked off the bones. You could see the skull beneath. My grandfather never forgot that.

They placed Anders on a stretcher and covered his head with a cloth. As the priest walked in front, leading the way and saying the burial prayer, they carried the body. But as they finished the first verse of the psalm, one of the men at the front dropped the stretcher. The others turned to look—and saw that the cloth had slipped off. Anders's eyes were open and staring, with nothing left to close them.

They couldn't take it. The priest quickly covered his face again, called for a shovel, and they buried him right there in the woods."

The next morning, Mr. Wraxall wrote that the deacon showed up soon after breakfast and took him to the church and the mausoleum. He noticed that the key to the tomb was hanging on a nail next to the pulpit. Since the church door was usually left unlocked, he figured it would be easy to come back on his own later if he wanted to take a closer look.

Inside the mausoleum, he was surprised by how grand it was. The room was filled with large, fancy tombs from the 1600s and 1700s. The carvings, decorations, and family symbols were detailed and impressive. In the center stood three copper coffins, each beautifully decorated. Two had large metal crosses on top, which was normal for Swedish and Danish graves. The third, belonging to Count Magnus, was different. Instead of a cross, it had a full-body engraving of the Count. Around the edges of the lid were bands of pictures showing different scenes.

One band showed a battle—with cannons firing, soldiers marching, and towns under attack. Another showed someone being executed. A third showed a man running through the woods, his hair flying and arms stretched out like he was terrified. Behind him was a strange figure. It wasn't clear if the artist had tried and failed to draw a person or had meant for it to look creepy on purpose. Since the rest of the artwork was so well done, Wraxall guessed the scary design was intentional.

The figure was oddly short and covered in a long, hooded robe that dragged along the ground. Only one part of its body stuck out, and it didn't look like a hand or arm. Wraxall thought it looked more like the tentacle of an octopus.

Looking at the image, he thought, "This must be symbolic—maybe it shows a monster chasing a soul. Maybe that's where the old story about Count Magnus and his mysterious companion comes from. Let's see what the hunter looks like. I bet it's a demon blowing a horn."

But it wasn't. The hunter was just a man in a cloak, standing on a small hill with a walking stick, watching what was happening. The artist had drawn him in a way that suggested he was calmly observing.

Wraxall also noticed that Count Magnus's coffin was locked with three thick steel padlocks. Two were still in place, but one had fallen to the floor. Not wanting to take up the deacon's time or delay his own work, Wraxall left the church and walked back to the manor.

Later, he wrote, "It's strange how when you walk a path often, you stop paying attention to where you're going. Tonight, just like before, I was so lost in thought—planning a secret visit to copy the tomb's inscriptions—that I didn't notice anything around me until I found myself at the churchyard gate again. I think I was singing something like, 'Are you awake, Count Magnus? Are you asleep, Count Magnus?' Maybe more, but I don't remember. I must've been saying it out loud without realizing."

He found the key where he expected and returned to the mausoleum. He copied most of the inscriptions he wanted and stayed until the daylight began to fade.

"I guess I was mistaken earlier," he wrote. "I thought only one padlock was loose, but now I see that two of them aren't locked. I picked them up and placed them gently on the window ledge, but I couldn't figure out how to close them again. The third one is still firmly locked. I think it works with some kind of spring, but I don't know how to open it. Honestly, if I had managed to unlock it, I probably would've opened the coffin. I can't explain it, but I feel strangely drawn to this old and serious nobleman."

The next day turned out to be his last at Råbäck. He got letters about money matters that made it clear he had to return to England. His research was almost done anyway, and traveling took time, so he decided to leave.

Still, saying goodbye and finishing his notes took longer than expected. The family invited him to stay for dinner, which they had at three in the afternoon, and it wasn't until almost 6:30 that he finally walked through the gates of the estate.

As he walked beside the lake one last time, he paid close attention to every detail, wanting to remember the peaceful beauty of the place. When he reached the top of the hill near the churchyard, he stopped and stood for several minutes, looking out at the dark woods beneath a soft green sky. Just before leaving, he felt like he couldn't go without saying goodbye to Count

Magnus too. The church was close, and he knew where the key was.

Soon, he was once again standing in front of Count Magnus's copper coffin, speaking to himself out loud like he often did. "You might've been a real scoundrel in your day, Magnus," he said, "but still, I think I'd like to see you, or maybe—"

Right then, something hit his foot. He stepped back quickly, and something dropped to the floor with a loud clang. It was the third and final padlock from the sarcophagus. He bent down to pick it up—and swore later that this was the honest truth—before he even stood up, he heard metal hinges creaking. The lid was starting to rise.

Maybe he panicked, but he didn't care. He ran. He got out of that tomb faster than he could even say a word. And what scared him even more was that once outside, he couldn't get the key to turn in the lock.

Now, sitting in his room and writing all of this down—barely twenty minutes after it happened—he asked himself if he had still heard the creaking noise as he ran. He wasn't sure. He just knew something had frightened him deeply, but whether it was something he saw or heard, he couldn't remember.

Then he wrote one last line:

"What have I done?"

***

Poor Mr. Wraxall. He left for England the next day, just as he had planned, and he arrived home safely. But judging by his messy handwriting and confused notes, it was clear he came back a changed man—troubled and deeply disturbed.

One of the small notebooks found with his belongings doesn't explain everything, but it gives some clues about what happened to him. Most of his return trip was by canal boat, and in this notebook, he tried several times to make a list of the people traveling with him. He attempted it at least six times, and each time his notes felt uneasy and nervous. The entries looked something like this:

"24. Pastor from a village in Skåne. Wears a black coat and soft black hat.

25. Salesman from Stockholm going to Trollhättan. Black cloak, brown hat.

26. Man in a long black cloak and wide-brimmed hat. Very old-fashioned."

That last entry was crossed out, with a note beside it: "Might be the same as No. 13. Still haven't seen his face." When checking entry 13, Wraxall had written it was a Roman Catholic priest wearing a traditional robe.

No matter how many times he counted, the result was always the same. There were twenty-eight people listed, and two stood out: one was a man in a long black cloak with a wide hat, and the other was a small figure in a dark hooded cloak.

But when it came time to eat, Wraxall always counted just twenty-six people at the table. Sometimes the man in the black cloak was missing—but the small hooded figure was never there.

***

When Mr. Wraxall arrived in England, it seems he landed at Harwich and immediately decided to get far away from someone—or maybe more than one person—who he never named, but clearly believed were following him. Instead of taking the train, which he didn't trust, he hired a closed carriage and rode across the countryside to the village of Belchamp St. Paul.

It was around nine in the evening, with a bright August moon lighting the sky, when he got close to the village. He sat at the front of the carriage, looking out the window. The fields and trees rushed by in the dark, quiet scenery. Then they reached a crossroads. At the corner stood two still figures. Both were wearing dark cloaks. One was tall and wore a wide-brimmed hat, the other shorter with a hood. He didn't have time to see their faces, and they didn't move at all—but the horse suddenly panicked, reared up, and bolted into a run. Mr. Wraxall dropped back into his seat, overwhelmed with fear. He had seen those two figures before.

When he finally got to Belchamp St. Paul, he was lucky enough to find a decent furnished room to rent. For the next day, things seemed quiet, almost peaceful. He used that time to write a few final notes, but they were scattered and panicked—too broken to share word for word. Still, it's easy to understand the message behind them.

He believed the people—or things—he feared were coming for him. He didn't know when or how, but he felt sure they would arrive. Again and again, he wrote, "What has he done?" and "Is there no hope?"

He knew doctors would say he was insane. The police wouldn't believe a word of it. The local priest was away. And so, in the end, he locked his door—and begged God for help.

***

People in Belchamp St. Paul still remember the night, years ago in August, when a strange man showed up in the village. Two mornings later, he was found dead. There was an investigation, and when the jury came to see the body, seven of them fainted. None of them would say what they saw. The official cause of death was listed as "an act of God." The family living in the house packed up and left that same week. They never came back.

As far as I know, no one ever found out what really happened. Most people believe it's a mystery that will never be solved.

Last year, the little house ended up in my hands through an inheritance. It had been empty since 1863, and no one was interested in living there. I chose to have it torn down. That's when we found the papers I've been telling you about—tucked away in a hidden cupboard under the window in the nicest bedroom.

The End

Thank You for Reading

Dear Reader,

We hope this timeless classic has sparked your imagination and enriched your literary journey. Now that you've turned the final page, we want to share a vision for the future of reading—one where every classic you've ever wanted to explore is at your fingertips, in a format that best suits your life.

We'd like to invite you to gain immediate, unlimited digital & audiobook access to hundreds of the most treasured literary classics ever written—along with the option to secure deluxe paperback, hardcover & box set editions at printing cost. Together, we can spark a new global literary renaissance alongside our small, independent publishing house called "The Library of Alexandria."

Thousands of years ago, the Library of Alexandria stood as a beacon of knowledge—until it was lost to history. We aim to reignite that spirit of preservation and discovery right now, in the modern age—only this time, it's accessible to all, in every language and every format.

Picture a world where every timeless classic, novel, poem, or philosophical treatise is not only available to read but also updated for today's readers—modernized, translated into any language or dialect, and ready to enjoy in any format you choose, whether that is in an eBook, audiobook, paperback, or deluxe hardcover & box set version a printing cost.

By joining our movement to rebuild the modern Library of Alexandria, you become part of an unprecedented mission to offer:

- **Unlimited Audiobook & eBook Access to the Greatest Classics of All Time**

  Instantly explore thousands of legendary works, from Plato and Shakespeare to Jane Austen and Leo Tolstoy. All are instantly ready to read or listen to, giving you a complete literary universe at your fingertips.

- **Paperback & Deluxe Editions at Printing Costs:**

  Purchase any title in a paperback, deluxe hardbound, or deluxe boxset edition at printing costs, shipped right to your doorstep. Curate your personal library of Alexandria with editions worthy of display—crafted to last, designed to captivate, and delivered straight to your door.

- **Modern translations for Contemporary Readers in all languages and dialects**

  Discover a vast selection of classics reimagined in clear, current language—no more struggling with outdated phrases or obscure references. Next to the original versions, we aim to offer translations in as many languages and dialects as possible.

  As we continue our translation efforts and add new languages, readers everywhere can connect with these works as if they were written today. By bridging linguistic divides, you're contributing to ensuring that these timeless stories become more meaningful, accessible, and inspiring for people across the globe.

- **Your Personal Library of Alexandria:**

  Over the months and years, you'll curate a unique physical archive of classics—each volume a testament to your taste, curiosity, and love of knowledge. It's not just about owning books—it's about curating a cultural legacy you'll cherish and pass down for generations to come.

- **Join a Global Literary Renaissance:**

  Your support fuels an ongoing mission: allowing us to reinvest in offering deluxe print editions (including special boxsets) at their true cost, broaden the range of available formats and translations, and extend the reach of these works to new audiences worldwide. By joining today, you're not just preserving a legacy of masterpieces; you set in motion a powerful wave of literary accessibility.

We are more than a publisher—we're a movement, and we can't do it alone. Your support lets us scale our mission, preserving and reimagining history's greatest works for tomorrow's readers.

Become a Torchbearer of knowledge.

Thank you for picking up this book and allowing us into your literary journey. As you turn the pages, know that you're part of something larger: a global effort to keep these stories alive, share their wisdom across borders and generations, and spark a true cultural revival for the modern era.

If this resonates with you—please consider taking the next step by visiting:

www.libraryofalexandria.com

With gratitude and a shared love of knowledge,

The Modern Library of Alexandria Team

Visit:

www.libraryofalexandria.com

Or scan the code below: